First published in Great Britain 1991
by Hamish Hamilton Ltd
Published 1993 by Mammoth
an imprint of Egmont Children's Books
Michelin House, 81 Fulham Road, London SW3 6RB

10 9 8 7 6 5

ISBN 0 7497 1021 7

A CIP catalogue record for this title
is available from the British Library

Printed in the U.A.E.

TARZANNA!
Babette Cole

Tarzanna lived in the jungle

with the animals.

One day she saw a
new kind of animal
she hadn't seen before

so she carried it off!

The new animal was
a boy called
Gerald.

He was studying
spiders.

Tarzanna taught him to speak animalese.
He taught her English.
"Why don't you visit my country?" said Gerald.
"O.K." said Tarzanna.

The animals did not want Tarzanna to go.

But she wanted to ride
in the helicopter.

Tarzanna didn't like Gerald's country!

Gerald's mum and dad were nice. They knew she missed the animals so they promised to take her to the zoo.

This was a serious mistake…

because she and Gerald could speak animalese.
"Let us out, Tarzanna!" said the animals.

So later, when it got dark

that's exactly what Tarzanna and Gerald did!

They took them back
to the flat...

but Gerald's mum just couldn't stand his spiders!

Tarzanna, Gerald and the animals ran away.

They hid out in the poshest boxes they could find. But the snooty shoppers were scared stiff!

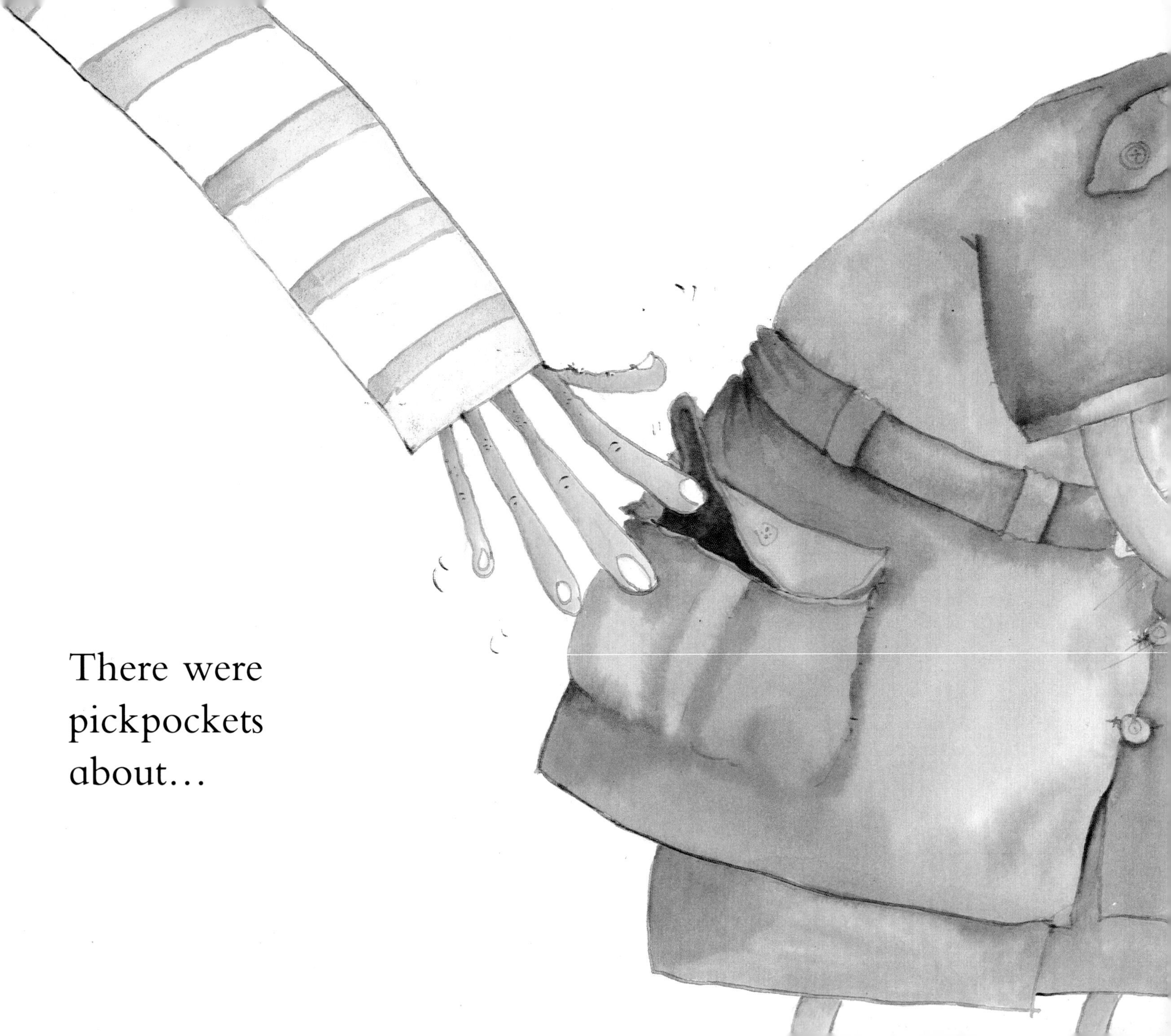

There were
pickpockets
about…

…but they didn't like what
was in Gerald's pocket!

"This is an awful way to live," complained Gerald. "The animals will start eating people if they don't get some dinner soon."

"We'll go and ask the Prime Minister," said Tarzanna. "He'll know what to do."

But the Prime Minister was
a bit tied up at the time!

Tarzanna, Gerald and the animals rescued the Prime Minister!

"Lucky the animals were so hungry," Tarzanna said.

Mmmmmm

When the fuss was over, Gerald's parents came for Tarzanna and Gerald...

...and the zoo man came for the animals!

"Wait!" commanded the Prime Minister
in a muffled voice.
"Everyone can go back
to the jungle!"

He bought them all first-class tickets home on Jungle Airways

The jungle animals loved
the zoo animals and
Gerald's dad built
a smashing
tree house.

"Doesn't your mum
mind the spiders?"
asked Tarzanna.

"I told her there wouldn't be any *spiders* in the bath in the jungle! said Gerald.